To Lucy

Happy 5th Birthday x x

SHARING

Carol Andrea Prodromou

AuthorHouse™ UK
1663 Liberty Drive
Bloomington, IN 47403 USA
www.authorhouse.co.uk
UK TFN: 0800 0148641 (Toll Free inside the UK)
UK Local: 02036 956322 (+44 20 3695 6322 from outside the UK)

Because of the dynamic nature of the Internet, any web addresses or links contained in this book may have changed since publication and may no longer be valid. The views expressed in this work are solely those of the author and do not necessarily reflect the views of the publisher, and the publisher hereby disclaims any responsibility for them.

This book is printed on acid-free paper.

ISBN: 979-8-8230-8061-3 (sc)
ISBN: 979-8-8230-8060-6 (e)

Print information available on the last page.

Published by AuthorHouse 02/10/2023

authorHOUSE®

SHARING

Annabelle Apple

Poppy Pear

Peter Pineapple

Olivia Orange

Bobby Banana

Simon Strawberry

Acknowledgements

I would like to express my deepest gratitude to my talented daughter, Cleo-Anne Ioannou who designed and drew the illustrations for my first book "Sharing"

I am so grateful to her for spending time to illustrate my book so beautifully and creatively, and for all her support on my journey.

I could not have undertaken this journey without you.

On a very cold morning, Annabelle Apple wanted to go to the store to buy some soup because she was very cold.

She left her house and while walking she bumped into Poppy Pear. "Where are you going?" asked Poppy Pear, Annabelle Apple said "I am going to buy soup from the store because it is very cold" Poppy Pear said "Can I come too?" and Annabelle Apple said "YES!"

As they were walking to the store they bumped into Peter Pineapple. They told him where they were going and he said "Can I come too?". They both said "YES!"

A little further down the road they saw Olivia Orange who asked, "Where are you going?" so they told her and she said "Can I come too?" and they said "YES!"

Not long after that Bobby Banana saw them, ran after them and said "Can I come too?" and they all said "YES!"

They almost reached the store and they all bumped into Simon Strawberry. "Where are you going?" he asked, they all said "We are going to the store to buy some soup because it is very cold. Simon Strawberry said "Can I come too?" and they all said "YES!"

They arrived at the store and went in to buy some soup, but there was not enough soup for everyone. So Annabelle Apple said "I will buy the soup and you can all come to my house and we can share it"

So that is what they did. They were
so grateful to Annabelle Apple for
sharing her soup with them all.

Annabelle Apple

Poppy Pear

Peter Pineapple

Olivia Orange

Bobby Banana

Simon Strawberry

Lightning Source UK Ltd.
Milton Keynes UK
UKHW051144150223
417029UK00002B/51